DISNEY

Beauty and the Beast

Autumn
Publishing

Once upon a time, an old beggar woman arrived at the castle of a handsome prince and offered him a rose in exchange for shelter.

However, the prince was unkind and turned her away. The old woman told him not to judge people on their appearance, but the prince just laughed.

Suddenly, the old woman transformed into a beautiful enchantress. To punish the prince, she cursed the castle and all who lived there. The only way to break the spell was for the prince to fall in love and be loved in return.

If this did not happen before the last petal fell from her rose, he would remain a beast forever.

In a sleepy village nearby, an eccentric inventor named Maurice lived with his beautiful daughter, Belle.

Gaston, a strong and handsome young man from the village, had decided that he wanted to make Belle his wife.

"After all," he told his friend LeFou, "she's the best-looking girl in town."

Gaston arrived at Belle's house, confident that Belle would agree to marry him. But when he asked her, Belle refused him without a second thought.

She knew she could never marry someone as arrogant and conceited as Gaston!

One day, Maurice set off for a fair with his latest invention. As night fell, he lost his way and had to seek refuge in the Beast's castle.

Maurice was welcomed by some friendly, enchanted servants, including a candelabra named Lumiere, a clock named Cogsworth, a teapot named Mrs Potts and her son Chip, a teacup.

But the Beast was furious when he discovered a stranger in his home and he threw Maurice into the dungeon. When Maurice's horse returned home alone, Belle set off at once to search for her father.

"Oh, Papa," Belle cried when she found Maurice in the freezing dungeon, "we must get you out of here!"

Sensing danger, Belle turned round. There was the Beast, towering over her and growling loudly.

"Please let my father go," Belle pleaded. "I'll take his place here."

The Beast agreed at once. He dragged Maurice out of the cell and sent him back to the village.

The Beast showed Belle to her room. "You can go anywhere in the castle," he told her, "except the West Wing. That is forbidden!"

Poor Belle was miserable. She missed her father and her home. The enchanted objects prepared a wonderful meal for her and tried to cheer her up with their singing and dancing.

But Belle was still lonely, and later that night she wandered through the castle. She soon found herself in the West Wing.

There, among broken furniture and cracked mirrors, she found the magic rose, its petals drooping sadly.

Just as Belle reached out to touch the rose, the Beast burst in, howling with rage. Terrified, Belle ran out into the snowy night.

Belle leapt onto her father's horse and set off blindly into the dark forest.

Suddenly, she was surrounded by a pack of vicious, hungry wolves. Just as the wolves closed in around her, the Beast appeared through the trees. Fighting bravely, he drove the wolves away.

But then the Beast sank to the ground in pain.

The wolves had injured him! Belle knew she could not leave him there alone.

She took the Beast back to the castle and gently tended his bleeding wounds. He seemed quite different now and Belle was no longer frightened of him.

Meanwhile, at the village tavern, Gaston was still brooding over Belle, even though his friends did their best to cheer him up. Suddenly, the door burst open and Maurice raced in.

"Help!" he cried. "Belle is being held prisoner by a monstrous beast!"

The men in the tavern burst out laughing. They thought Maurice was mad! But Gaston smiled to himself. He had thought of a way to make Belle marry him!

He called a tall, sinister-looking man from the asylum over to his table and began to tell him what he had in mind.

As the days passed, Belle and the Beast spent more and more time together. The enchanted servants were delighted. They were certain that Belle would fall in love with their master and break the spell. But time was running out. Each day, more petals fell from the magic rose.

One evening, after dining and dancing together, the Beast and Belle sat out on the terrace in the cool night air.

"Are you happy here, Belle?" asked the Beast.

"Yes," replied Belle. "I just wish I could see my father again."

"You can," said the Beast and he gave Belle a magic mirror. "This will show you whatever you wish."

"Oh, thank you!" exclaimed Belle. But as she gazed into it, Belle saw her father lost and trembling with cold as he searched for her!

Although the Beast loved Belle, he knew he had to let her go to her father. "Take the mirror with you," he said, sadly, "so you can remember me."

Belle set off from the castle and soon found Maurice. She brought him safely home and put him to bed.

The next day, Gaston arrived at Belle's house with a crowd of villagers. He said that Maurice would be taken to an asylum unless Belle agreed to marry him.

"My father's not mad!" cried Belle.

"He must be," said LeFou. "He was raving about a monstrous beast!"

"The Beast is real!" cried Belle. "Look!" She held up the magic mirror and the crowd saw the Beast for themselves.

They all shouted with fear and refused to listen to Belle when she told them the Beast was kind and good.

The men marched up to the castle doors and broke them down. Cogsworth led the enchanted servants in a brave defence of the castle. But the Beast missed Belle and was too heartbroken to fight, even when Gaston beat him with a club and forced him onto the castle roof.

Only when he heard Belle's voice did the Beast look up.
"You came back!" he cried, rushing to embrace Belle.
This was the chance Gaston had been waiting for. Drawing
his dagger, he stabbed the Beast in the back. But as the Beast
collapsed, Gaston tripped and fell tumbling from the roof.

Belle ran to the wounded Beast and bent to kiss him.
The last petal was just about to fall from the rose.
"You can't die," sobbed Belle. "I love you! I wish I had
never left you alone!"

Suddenly, a magic mist surrounded the Beast and, before
Belle's astonished eyes, he changed into the handsome young
prince he had once been.

One by one, the enchanted servants became human again.
Weeping with joy, they hugged each other as the prince swept
Belle into his arms.

The prince had found his true love at last and the spell of the enchantress was broken. As the sun burst through the clouds, they knew they would all live happily ever after.